This igloo book belongs to:

....

Contents

Published in 2011
by Igloo Books Ltd
Cottage Farm
Sywell
Northants
NN6 0BJ
www.igloo-books.com

10 9 8 7 6 5 4 3 2 1
ISBN: 978-0-85734-498-4

Printed and manufactured in China
Illustrated by Hannah Wood
Stories by Melanie Joyce

Stories
for 6
Year
Olds

igloo

What are you doing, Dennis?

It was a lovely, sunny day. "Shall we go for a picnic?" asked Dad. "Yes, please," replied Dennis and he ran off to rummage in the cupboard under the stairs. There was a clinking and clanging and a great deal of noisy pulling and tugging.

   "What are you doing, Dennis?" said Mum, as she packed up the picnic basket with lots of treats.
"Nothing," said Dennis, closing his rucksack and grabbing his boots.

Soon, everyone was in the car. "Ready?" asked Dad.
"Ready," said Mum and Dennis and his little sister, Lola.

Dennis reached into his rucksack. There was a chinking and a clinking and a strange, papery rustling. "What are you doing, Dennis?" whispered Lola. "Nothing," replied Dennis, with a mysterious smile, as the car rumbled off into the sunny countryside.

Soon, Dad found the perfect spot for a picnic. "Here we are," he said.
Dennis dashed off to explore. But, Mum said, "Dennis, can you play with Lola
while we get the picnic ready?"

Dennis didn't want to play dollies with Lola, it was boring. Then, suddenly,
he noticed something wiggly and slippery, sliding in the soil.

"Come on, Lola," said Dennis. "We're going to play a very special game." Dennis rummaged in his rucksack. He pulled out his big, magnifying glass. "Ah, ha!" said Dennis. "Look what I've found."

"Let me see," said Lola, and she crouched down to have a look. "Ugh," said Lola, "it's big, fat ugly-wuggly snake!"

"It's only a worm," said Dennis. But Lola had already run off across the grass.
"What are you doing, Dennis," called out Mum.
"Nothing," said Dennis, as he followed his little sister.

Dennis saw something hopping over the grass. "Ah, ha!" he said, holding up his magnifying glass. "Look what I've found, Lola."
"Let me see," said Lola and she bent down to have a look. Two, enormous eyes stared out from a green, shiny face. Then suddenly, the face hopped off on two enormous legs, BOING!

"Aargh," cried Lola, "it's coming to get me!"
"It's alright, Lola," said Dennis, "it's only a frog." But Lola had run off.
"What are you doing, Dennis?" shouted Dad.
"Nothing," said Dennis and he chased after his little sister.

In a leafy hedge, a spider had spun his web and was sitting right in the middle of it. So, Dennis showed Lola with his big magnifying glass.

Lola stared, at the long, hairy legs and the big, hairy body. "It's a monster," she cried. Then, suddenly, the big web wobbled and the huge spider moved. "The monster's going to eat us!" shrieked Lola. "I want my mummy." Just then, Mum called out, "The picnic's ready."

9

"Mummy, Mummy!" cried Lola, running over. "I've seen a wiggly worm
and a hopping frog and a monster that moved. He was as big as a house and
he nearly got me!"

"Don't worry, Lola," soothed Mum, "there aren't really any monsters. It's just
Dennis playing a game with you."

10

"What have you been saying to your little sister?" asked Dad.
"Nothing," said Dennis, slipping his magnifying glass back into his rucksack.
He sat down and looked at all the delicious food on the picnic rug.
Then, Dennis gave a small smile and took a big bite of his favourite
sort of sandwich.

Brave Bonny

One day, Bonny was helping her Dad to prepare a party for Olly's birthday. Suddenly, outside, thunder crashed and lightning flashed. "I don't like it," said Bonny, and she covered her ears and began to cry.

"Bonny's a cry-baby and she's not brave," teased her little brother, Olly. "That's not true, Olly," said Dad, "just because Bonny is afraid, it doesn't mean she isn't brave."

That afternoon, everyone came round for the party. There were sandwiches and jelly and lots of party games. Bonny forgot all about the thunderstorm. She was having a lovely time when suddenly, there was a very loud, BANG!

With one great leap, Bonny dived under the table, making the jellies wobble and the plates clatter. "Silly, Bonny," giggled Olly, "it's just a balloon bursting." Poor Bonny felt very silly.

13

The next day, Dad took Bonny and Olly to the funfair. That made Bonny feel a lot better. She loved the merry-go-round and the spinning tea-cups. "I bet you're too scared to go on the ghost train," said Olly. "No, I'm not," replied Bonny, stomping over to the ghost train.

14

The ghost train was creepy and covered in cobwebs. There were strange, ghoulish figures who let out long moans and rattled their chains. "I don't like it," wailed Bonny. "I want to get off." She stuffed her head underneath Dad's woolly jumper.

"I'm not brave at all," sobbed Bonny, as the little cart trundled back out into the sunlight.
"Never mind," said Dad. "Let's go to the park instead."

At the park, Dad chatted to a friend while Olly and Bonny had fun on the climbing frame. Then, Bonny whizzed round on the roundabout and swung on the monkey bars. It was such fun, she forgot all about the ghost train. Then, suddenly, Bonny noticed three older boys crowding round Olly. He looked very worried.

Suddenly, Bonny felt strangely hot and bothered and she began to trot over to Olly. Then she ran, as fast as she could, right into the middle of the little group.

"What are you doing?" she snorted. "Leave my little brother alone!" The bullies moved back because Bonny looked very angry.

"They wouldn't let me play in the sandpit," said Olly. "They said it was theirs."
"Well it isn't," replied Bonny. "It is for everyone to play in." Then, she took
Olly by the hand and led him back to Dad.

Dad was very proud of Bonny for sticking up for her little brother.
"Well," said Dad, "I think Bonny was very brave, don't you, Olly?" he asked.
"Yes," said Olly, giving Bonny a big hug. "I'm sorry I laughed at you when
you were afraid," he said. "I think you're the bravest sister ever."

Dinky's Great Escape

Josh and Amy were looking after Dinky the hamster for the night.
"Make sure he has some food, water and fresh bedding," said Mum. "Aunty's coming to stay and I don't want Dinky running around, so remember to keep his cage door closed."
"We will," said Amy and Josh and they took Dinky upstairs.

20

Just then, the door bell rang, ding-dong.
"That must be Aunty," said Amy. "I wonder if she's brought us any presents?"
The twins rushed downstairs, but, they had forgotten to shut Dinky's cage door.

21

Aunty made a great fuss of Amy and Josh and they forgot all about Dinky. They were too busy opening presents and eating cakes and having fun.

Later on, when it was time for bed, everyone went upstairs. Aunty unpacked her suitcase and the twins went to their room. That's when they noticed that Dinky had gone.

Amy and Josh looked in the cupboards and under the bed. They looked in the wardrobe and the laundry basket and even in the sock drawer. But, Dinky was nowhere to be found. "Where is he?" whispered Josh. Suddenly, there was a loud scream from Aunty's bedroom.

Across the hallway, Aunty was jumping up and down on her bed.
"I saw something furry dash past my door!" she cried. "Maybe it's a
mouse, or a rat."
"Or a hamster," whispered Mum, as she glared at Amy and Josh.

"Don't worry, Aunty," said Mum. "I'm sure there's nothing to worry about.
You settle down and have a good night's sleep."

Josh and Amy went back to their bedroom to get ready for bed.
"My slippers have got holes in," said Josh.
"My nightdress has got holes in, too," said Amy, "Dinky must have got
hungry, but couldn't get back into his cage." Amy thought they had better go
and tell Mum — because Dinky might eat the whole house.

As always, Mum knew exactly what to do. "We'll have to search everywhere that we can think of," she whispered. "But, be very quiet. We don't want to wake Aunty."

So, Mum, Josh and Amy crept all over the house. They looked in every nook and cranny and dark corner and shadowy place. But Dinky was nowhere to be found.

Then, just as they were about to give up and go to bed, Amy heard a rustling and a scratching and a strange sort of nibbling. "It's coming from Aunty's bedroom," Mum whispered.

Mum opened the door, very carefully, and there was Dinky, happily munching Aunty's best hat.

"Quickly!" said Mum. "Go and get some of Dinky's hamster nuts."
So, Josh went off and got some nuts. When he came back, Mum crept,
very carefully, into Aunty's room and laid a trail of nuts all the way
back to Josh and Amy's bedroom.

Soon, Dinky was safely back in his cage. Mum smiled at Amy and Josh. "Off to bed, you two," she said. "And next time, remember to close Dinky's door." Amy and Josh promised that they would. Then, they settled down for a good night's sleep.

The Pirate Princess

Amber was at the theme park with her Dad and little brother, Timmy.
"Can we go on the ghost train?" she asked.
"In a minute," replied Dad, "let Timmy go on a ride first."

Amber didn't want to wait. So, she huffed and puffed, in an impatient sort of way, and looked around. That's when she noticed something amazing.

It was an enormous, black pirate ship. "Wow," said Amber.
I've always wanted to go on a real pirate ship.

Just then, a big voice boomed out, "All aboard the Jolly Dolphin.
Captain Crossbone's my name and I'm sailing for Treasure Island."

Amber looked round to check that Dad was still busy watching Timmy
on the merry-go-round.

"I'll just have a look at the ship," thought Amber, "I won't be long." And she climbed up the ramp of the Jolly Dolphin.

On board, Captain Crossbone stood with his arms folded. He had an eye-patch and a big parrot sitting on his shoulder.
"Shiver me timbers!" he cried. "We have a pirate princess aboard!"
The big parrot squawked, "*Princess, princess,*" and all the other pirates laughed.

"Actually, I just came to have a look," said Amber. But, before she had time to say anymore, Captain Crossbone took a big, deep breath and bellowed at the top of his voice, "Hoist the mainsail, anchor's away!"

Suddenly, the Jolly Dolphin began to move. "Oh, dear," said aweigh, as she saw Dad and Timmy grow smaller and smaller. "It looks like I'm going to Treasure Island!"

Captain Crossbone gave Amber a proper pirate hat and boots. She even had her own special sword. "That's for fighting bad pirates," he winked.

Suddenly, someone called out, "Land ahoy."
"It's Treasure Island," said the captain. "Ssh, be quiet now, we have to creep ashore, in case the treasure thieves are looking to plunder our loot. They're a fiercesome bunch, make no mistake."

So, Amber, Captain Crossbone and the crew of the Jolly Dolphin crept over the sand and into a cave where everything was quiet.

In the middle of the cave was a gigantic chest. It was full of shiny, gold treasure that spilled over the sides and onto the floor. They were just about to carry it away when there was a very scary sound.

Fierce-looking, raggedy pirates ran out from the rocks. "Give us the treasure!" they cried, waving their swords in the air.

"Quick, take the treasure and run for the ship!" cried Captain Crossbone. So, Amber grabbed handfuls of jewels and glittering gems. She ran as fast as she could, out of the cave and over the sand, with the nasty pirates hot on her heels.

After a lot of sploshing and splashing, the treasure was safely on board. "Phew," said Amber. "I'm all out of breath, but that was brilliant fun." "You're a very brave pirate princess," said Captain Crossbone. The crew of the Jolly Dolphin agreed and they shouted and cheered.

Then, Captain Crossbone took another big breath and bellowed, "Cast off, steady as she goes, it's time to head home."

Amber said goodbye to Captain Crossbone and skipped off the
Jolly Dolphin, just in time to see Dad taking Timmy off the merry-go-round.
"Where have you been, Amber?" asked Dad. "I looked round and you were gone."

Amber told Dad that she just went on board the Jolly Dolphin to have a
look around. She thought it best not to mention Captain Crossbone,
or the amazing Treasure Island.

38

"I'm sure you were curious about the ship," said Dad. "But you mustn't go off without telling me." Then, he smiled and put his arm round Amber. "Come on," he said. "I'll take you on the ghost train."

"Alright," said Amber, smiling to herself. It would be fun to go on the ghost train. But it wouldn't be nearly as exciting as being a pirate princess on the Jolly Dolphin.

Uncle Percy's Potions

Jake and Emily had never been to Uncle Percy's house before. It was huge and creepy. "Make sure you don't get into any trouble," said Mum and Dad, as Uncle Percy showed them into the hallway.

   "Please can we explore?" asked Jake.
"Yes," replied Uncle Percy in his deep, gruff voice. "But be careful. This is a very old house and it has many secrets. We don't want you getting lost."

"Don't worry, we won't," said Jake, and he led Emily off along a corridor that had threadbare carpets and locked, wooden doors. "I wonder what's behind them?" said Emily.

"Maybe monsters?" whispered Jake. "Maybe Uncle Percy's really a mad professor who does secret experiments that he doesn't want anyone to know about."

At the end of the corridor, was a small door. Jake turned the handle. With a soft click, the door slowly opened. Beyond it was a staircase leading downwards. "Where does it go?" asked Emily.

"I don't know," replied Jake, "but maybe it leads to the secret laboratory where Uncle Percy makes special potions."

Jake clicked his pocket torch on and, with Emily keeping close, they crept slowly down the winding, stone steps.

At the bottom, the pale beam of light fell on shelves stacked with bottles full of different-coloured liquids. "What are they?" asked Emily. "I think they're special potions!" gasped Jake.

Suddenly, there was a sort of thumping and clumping coming along the corridor. Then, with a creak, the little door opened and feet shuffled slowly down the steep, stone steps.

"Quick, hide," said Jake and he pulled Emily behind a dusty, old chest. *Shuffle, shuffle, clump* went the feet at the bottom of the steps. "Hmm..." said a gruff voice. "Now, which of my special bottles shall I choose tonight?" "It's Great Uncle Percy," whispered Jake. "I told you he was a mad professor!"

44

There were noisy chinks and clanks, as Uncle Percy took several bottles and made his way back up the stairs. At the top, he pulled the little door closed and locked it.

"I'm scared," said Emily. But Jake was busy looking at a metal lever, shaped liked a winged horse, that was sticking out of the wall. "I wonder what this does," he said, pushing the lever downwards.

The lever moved and suddenly a doorway opened from the stone wall.
"It's a secret passage," said Jake. "Come on, let's find out where it goes."

Jake and Emily crept through the long, dark tunnel that ended at some steps leading to a door.
"Drink up," said a voice from behind the door .
"It's Great Uncle Percy," whispered Jake. "He's giving his potions to Mum and Dad!"

Jake barged through the door into a room where Mum, Dad and Uncle Percy were sipping potions. "Don't drink it – it's a special potion and Uncle Percy's a mad professor!" shouted Jake.

Mum, Dad and Uncle Percy looked at each other and they looked at Jake. Then, they burst out laughing.

"I suppose you could call my famous blueberry cordial a special potion," chuckled Uncle Percy. "I make lots of other flavours, too. Would you like to try one?"

Jake and Emily felt really silly. They said sorry to Uncle Percy, for thinking he was a mad professor, and had a delicious drink of tangy, raspberry cordial. Then they tasted the peach flavour and the lemon and the blackberry, too. Discovering Uncle Percy's potions was the best thing ever.